First Little Readers™

My Silly Sandwich

by Liza Charlesworth

ISBN: 978-1-338-29798-0

Illustrated by Tammie Lyon

First printing, June 2018.

 Published by Scholastic Inc. Printed in Jiaxing, China.

Hi! I am Sid.
I like to make silly sandwiches.

This is my dog, Spot.
He likes to watch.

You are in luck!
I will make a silly sandwich
right now.

I put on lots of ham.

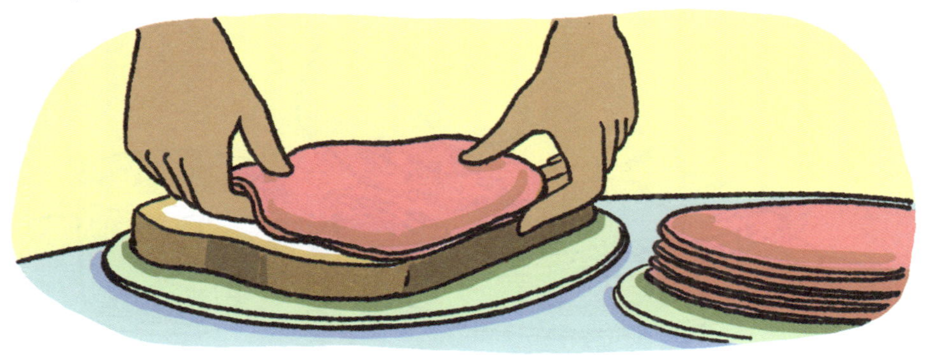

I put on lots of cheese.

I put on lots of pickles.

I put on lots of noodles.

I put on lots of jelly beans.

I put on lots of ketchup.

All done!
I told you my sandwich was silly.
Now, I will get some milk
to go with it.

I am back.
Hey!
Where did my sandwich go?

Did my mom eat it?
"No, your sandwiches
are too silly," she says.

Did my dad eat it?
"No, your sandwiches
are too silly," he says.

Did my sister eat it?
"No, your sandwiches
are too silly," she says.

Hey!
Who ate my sandwich?
Wait.
I see some crumbs.

I follow them.
Crumb, crumb, crumb.

Crumb, crumb, crumb.

Hey!
Spot ate my sandwich.
Now, that is too silly!